D0194791

ER   Deary, Terry
2-3
DEA   Lion's slave

EASY READER 2-3

Boulder Ci
701 A
Boulder   vard
DISCARD   RV 89005

THE
LION'S
SLAVE

Boulder City Library
70___ Boulevard
Bo___ DISCARD
NOV   2008

by Terry Deary

illustrated by Helen Flook

PICTURE WINDOW BOOKS
Minneapolis, Minnesota

Editor: Shelly Lyons
Page Production: Michelle Biedscheid
Art Director: Nathan Gassman
Associate Managing Editor: Christianne Jones

First American edition published in 2008 by
Picture Window Books
5115 Excelsior Boulevard
Suite 232
Minneapolis, MN 55416
877-845-8392
www.picturewindowbooks.com

First published in 2007 by A&C Black Publishers Limited, 38 Soho Square,
London W1D 3HB, with the title THE LION'S SLAVE.

Text copyright © 2007 Terry Deary
Illustrations copyright © 2007 Helen Flook

All rights reserved. No part of this book may be reproduced without
written permission from the publisher. The publisher takes no responsibility
for the use of any of the materials or methods described in this book, nor the
products thereof.

Printed in the United States of America.

 All books published by Picture Window Books
are manufactured with paper containing at least
10 percent post-consumer waste.

Library of Congress Cataloging-in-Publication Data
Deary, Terry.
The lion's slave / by Terry Deary ; illustrated by Helen Flook.
p. cm. — (Read-it! chapter books. Historical tales)
ISBN 978-1-4048-4050-8 (library binding)
1. Archimedes—Juvenile fiction. [1. Archimedes—Fiction.
2. Greece—History—To 146 B.C.—Fiction.] I. Flook, Helen, ill. II. Title.
PZ7.D3517Li 2008
[Fic]—dc22   2007038080

Table of Contents

Words to Know

Aesop—an ancient Greek storyteller whose fables teach a lesson

Archimedes—a famous Greek mathematician who lived from about 287 B.C. to about 212 B.C.

catapult—an ancient machine used for launching large rocks during battle

eureka—the word Archimedes shouted when he made a discovery

Syracuse—a Greek colony on the eastern side of the island of Sicily, in Italy

tunic—a long, belted shirt worn by ancient Greeks and Romans

Chapter One

The Lion
of Syracuse

Syracuse, 213 B.C.

Aesop the Greek storyteller said:
*You may share the work of the great, but
you will not share the rewards.*

My master liked to call me stupid.

"You are stupid, Lydia," he would say. "If you had twice as many brains, you would still be stupid."

That was a clever thing to say. Of course, my master, Archimedes, *was* the smartest man in all of Greece. If he called me stupid, then I must have been.

I cleaned his rooms,

washed his clothes,

cooked his meals,

and helped him test his machines.

Because Archimedes was a great inventor, people called him the Lion of Syracuse. And he often roared at me like a lion.

"I bet your brain feels as good as new, because you have never used it," he told me.

"Thank you, sir," I said.

I was clumsy. When I tried to dust the bottles and jars in his workshop, I often spilled them.

"You are a donkey, Lydia," he would say. "What did I call you?"

"A donkey, sir," I would answer.

There is a story about Archimedes taking a bath one day, long before I started working for him. When he sat down in the bathtub, the water overflowed onto the floor.

That gave him a mathematical idea that I have never understood. Anyway, Archimedes jumped out of the bathtub and ran down the street telling everyone.

"Eureka!" he cried. "Eureka" meant he had found the answer.

But Archimedes hadn't stopped to put on any clothes!

He often forgot about simple things like that. And I think it was his brilliant brain that later got him killed.

He thought everyone was as excited by his inventions as he was. He forgot that people have feelings. Some people even have feelings of revenge.

If he had been as stupid as I was, then he would still be alive today.

The trouble for Archimedes started when the Romans came to Syracuse.

The Romans
Arrive

"You are stupid, Lydia, stupid," Archimedes told me. "I don't know why I hired you. You must be a very cheap servant."

"I am more than cheap! You don't pay me anything at all," I reminded him.

"Then how do you live?" he asked.

"I eat a little of the food I cook for you, and I sleep on a straw bed in your attic," I answered.

"Huh!" he grumbled. "Then I still pay you too much."

"Yes, sir," I said.

On that day, the Romans arrived to attack us. Their ships floated in the cool, blue sea off the shore of Syracuse. Soldiers stood on the decks but didn't dare to come on land. Our soldiers on the walls would have shot them with arrows.

"Will the Romans kill us when they come ashore, sir?" I asked.

"Stupid child," Archimedes said. "You, Lydia, are a young and healthy girl. They will not kill you.

You are not worth it. They will take

you away and make you a slave. But then you will not have a kind master like me, will you?"

"No, sir," I said.

Archimedes' house stood on the top of a hill. We looked over the garden walls and down over the city walls to see the Roman ships shimmering in the heat. The sun was beating down on us, and I wished I could go swimming in the cool, blue sea.

"I would like to smash those ships," Archimedes said.

"You could throw rocks at them," I suggested.

He looked at me and mopped his bald, sweating head with a cloth.

"Stupid girl," he said.

"Can you do something about them?" I asked.

"Perhaps I could invent something," he said.

I clapped my hands and jumped on the dry, brown grass. "That would be marvelous, sir," I said. "You are a wonderful inventor. You invented a way to raise water out of a river and into the fields."

"Yes," he nodded. "They call it Archimedes' Screw."

"I'm sure you could invent a
machine to fire big rocks at those ships,"
I said.

My master shook his head. "Find me
a rock, and I'll show you why it's not
possible," he said.

There were no rocks in the garden because I kept it weeded and full of flowers. But there were some large ones in the field outside the garden wall.

"I'll get one from the field," I said.

Archimedes threw up his hands.

"Silly child. Those stones are too large for you to carry," he said.

"Then I'll throw one over the wall," I offered.

"If you can't pick it up, you can't throw it!" he replied in his lion's roar.

"Oh, throwing it is easier!" I answered as I laughed. Then I picked up the plank of wood that my master used as a garden seat, tucked it under my arm, and walked out into the field.

I placed the plank on a round stone
and let one end drop onto the ground.

I rolled a large rock onto that end.
Then I jumped onto the other end. The
rock shot up into the air.

I remember it to this day. And I really remember the way my master, Archimedes, screamed.

Chapter Three

Archimedes' Catapult

The rock soared into the cloudless sky. It looped over the wall and headed down into the garden. Well, it would have headed into the garden if my master hadn't been standing there. Instead, it curved toward his head.

My master doesn't have hair on his head like handsome, young Ajax, who lives on the main street. Ajax has fine hair that is parted down the middle of his beautiful head.

If my master's hair were like that, the rock would have parted it. Instead, the rock almost parted his head.

Archimedes ducked and scrambled out of the way, and the rock landed with a thump on the grass.

"Oops!" I said with a silly grin. "Sorry, sir!"

He didn't call me stupid. He was sputtering and moaning too much to call me anything.

I brought the plank back into the garden, made it into a seat again, and sat him down.

"You … you … ," he began.

"I know," I said. "I'm foolish."

He shook his head and continued,
"You … you … could … have … ."

"I could have fired a bigger rock, and
you would have seen it better," I added.

He shook his head. "You … you … could … have … killed me!" he yelled.

"Sorry, sir," I said. "It was a game I played with my brothers when we were younger. We used to use a small plank to fire balls of cloth into the air. Then we would see who could catch them. But I knew it would work for a rock, too."

He glared at me. "Why did you do that?" he demanded.

"Because you told me to find a rock for you," I answered.

"I did?" he asked.

"You did," I said.

"So I did! I was going to show you that it's impossible to throw big rocks at the Roman ships," he said.

"If you say so, sir," I muttered.

"But if I get a really long plank … ," he began.

"As long as a tree," I said.

"As long as a tree … then I could fire boulders big enough to sink those ships," he said.

I covered my mouth with my hand. "Oh, sir, that's brilliant!" I announced. "Oh, sir, I knew you'd invent something to save us! It's true what people say!"

"What do people say?" he asked.

"That you are the smartest man in Syracuse!" I answered.

Archimedes smiled and nodded. "I am the smartest man in Greece," he declared. "In fact, I'm the smartest man in the world!"

Chapter Four

Archimedes' Claw

You know what happened next, of course. It is written in the history books. Archimedes made his mighty throwing machines. He called them "catapults."

The Lord of Syracuse gathered the crowds in the main square. He stood at the window of the palace. "The people of Syracuse are blessed by the gods," he cried. "The Romans have their ships, but we have Archimedes—the Lion of Syracuse!"

And we all cheered until our throats
were sore.

"Roman ships have been sunk," the
Lord went on. "And the rest have been
driven out to sea. All thanks to the
great inventor, Archimedes!"

There were cheers and more cheers!

The next morning, I rose from my bed to make my master his breakfast. I found him in the garden, kneeling beside the pond. He was using a toy catapult to fire at toy ships in the pond.

"Would you like your breakfast, sir?"
I asked.

He waved me away with a hand.
When he was thinking his great
thoughts, no one else mattered.

"During the night, the Romans
sailed into our harbor," he said quickly.

"So? We can sink them with your great war machines," I said.

He took a pebble and placed it on the toy catapult. "Look," he said. "There is a Roman ship in the harbor. I fire a rock."

He fired. The rock landed in the middle of the pond and missed the little ship.

"So? We can move the catapult back!" I said.

"I've tried it, simple girl," he replied.

He moved the catapult back. He fired again. This time the rock landed on the edge of the pond.

"See?" he groaned. "It landed short of the harbor. If we get it wrong, we will shatter our own town. The Romans are clever. They know we can't fire at them when they are so close."

I looked at the models and picked up a twig from the garden. I took a thread from my tunic and dangled it from the twig. I took a pin and bent it.

"What are you doing, stupid girl?" Archimedes asked.

"When I was a child, I used to fish with my brothers," I said.

I dangled my little rod over the model ship and hooked it into the air. "If the Romans come too close, we could fish them out of the water!" I said as I laughed.

"Idiot child," he snapped. "We cannot build a mighty fishing rod. It's a stupid idea."

"I know, sir," I sighed.

Archimedes snapped his fingers.

"But if we built a tall crane," he murmured, taking the rod from my hand, "we could reach out over the harbor and grab the Roman ships. We could attach a claw on the end, like a crab's, and grab them! Eureka!"

I covered my mouth with my hand. "Oh, sir, that's brilliant!" I shouted. "Oh, sir, I knew you'd invent something to save us! It's true what people say!"

"What do people say?" he asked.

"That you are the smartest man in Syracuse!" I replied.

"We will call it Archimedes' Claw!" he announced.

Chapter Five

Archimedes' End

Archimedes' Claw smashed several
Roman ships and drove them back.

Again, the Lord of Syracuse gathered the people in the square and told them how great my master was. He paid Archimedes a fortune.

It was strange that his great mind took simple ideas and made them work as weapons of war. The ideas had come from games I used to play as a child.

I was too stupid to see how they could help us win the war. But I felt I was sharing in my master's work.

One day, I made a fire using a mirror that bent the sun's rays into a beam of scorching light.

Archimedes watched me and went off muttering.

The next day, my master had built a huge metal mirror that sent a hot ray of sun onto the Roman fleet. It set their ships on fire.

The Lord of Syracuse heaped more treasures on my master. I was so proud of him! I suppose, in a way, that is how I killed him. Well, I didn't take his life myself. But I was to blame. I was stupid.

You see, the Romans eventually came onto land. They ran through the town, punishing and killing people.

Finally, they reached our house at the top of the hill. My master was in the garden, planning something new. He was drawing circles in the dust with a stick.

A Roman soldier came up to the gate. "Who lives here?" he asked.

"My master, Archimedes, the Lion of Syracuse," I said proudly. I showed him through the garden to where Archimedes was scratching in the dirt.

The soldier sighed and said, "We've heard about him. General Marcellus said he is not to be harmed."

"Ah!" I said. "That's nice. Especially after all he did to you!"

The soldier stiffened. "Did? What do you mean, did?" he asked. "He does science and math. He's harmless, isn't he?"

"Ha! That's a good one," I laughed. "The great Archimedes invented the catapult that sank your ships."

"My friend died on one of those ships," the soldier growled, pulling out his sword.

"Then he invented Archimedes' Claw, and that wrecked more of your ships," I said and giggled.

"My brother died on one of those ships," the soldier fumed, raising his sword above his head.

"And, of course, he invented the burning mirror that scorched the ships," I finished.

"I was burned on the arm by that!" the soldier roared. He stepped toward my master and yelled, "Archimedes, you villain, come with me!"

My master waved him away. When he was thinking his great thoughts, no one else mattered. Then he said, "Don't disturb my circles."

These were his famous last words.
They were his last words because the
soldier brought down his sword with
the fury of a madman.

A Slave's Life

I know. I am stupid. I should not have told the soldier that Archimedes had invented the war machines.

I should have said, "I showed my master how the catapult worked. My fishing rod gave him the idea for the claw. And my mirror showed him how to make a deadly sunbeam."

But the soldier wouldn't believe that a stupid girl would have such ideas. Or, if I had said that, maybe he would have blamed me. Then he would have killed me! Maybe being stupid saved my life!

So that is the story of how the Lion of Syracuse's life ended. But what happened to the Lion's slave? What happened to me?

You won't be surprised to hear that my master was right. I became a Roman's slave. But it's not such a bad life. My new master is kind.

In fact, he's far kinder to me than old Archimedes, and he never calls me stupid!

I only wish my old master had shared some of his riches with me before he died. The Lord of Syracuse had given him a fortune for his clever machines. I got nothing, even though I sometimes think I helped create those inventions.

But then I remember Aesop once said, "You may share the work of the great, but you will not share the rewards."

Afterword

Archimedes lived in Greece from about 287 to 212 B.C. He was one of the smartest men in Greece. When the Greek colony of Syracuse was attacked, he really did invent war machines to help keep the Romans out. Today, we aren't sure all of his machines worked, but his ideas were very clever.

The story of Lydia helping with the inventions isn't true. But beginning in 215 B.C., Archimedes and his soldiers did keep the Romans out for three years.

By the time the Romans battled their way into Syracuse, they were pretty angry with Archimedes. But they knew Archimedes was a great man, and the Roman soldiers were told not to harm him.

Sadly, Archimedes was busy scratching

a math problem in the dust. He ignored the Roman soldier who was sent to find him. The soldier became furious and killed the helpless inventor. With one stroke of his sword, he destroyed one of the smartest men the world has ever known.

Archimedes was known as the Lion of Syracuse. Great men like Archimedes are remembered for thousands of years. But he couldn't have defeated the Romans on his own. He needed servants and soldiers to help him.

Archimedes held back the Romans with the help of hundreds of people. Most of those people are long forgotten.

It is true what Aesop said, "You may share the work of the great, but you will not share the rewards."

On the Web

FactHound offers a safe, fun way to find Web sites related to topics in this book. All of the sites on FactHound have been researched by our staff.

1. Visit *www.facthound.com*
2. Type in this special code:
   1404840508
3. Click on the FETCH IT button.

Your trusty FactHound will fetch the best sites for you!

Look for more *Read-It!* Reader Chapter Books: Historical Tales:

The Actor, the Rebel, and the Wrinkled Queen

The Blue Stone Plot

The Boy Who Cried Horse

The Gold in the Grave

The Lion's Slave

The Magic and the Mummy

The Maid, the Witch, and the Cruel Queen

The Phantom and the Fisherman

The Plot on the Pyramid

The Prince, the Cook, and the Cunning King

The Secret Warning

The Shepherd and the Racehorse

The Thief, the Fool, and the Big Fat King

The Torchbearer

The Tortoise and the Dare

The Town Mouse and the Spartan House